How Do Living Things Survive in Their Environment?

H.B. 64 2015-2017
Massillon Bd. of Ed.
St. Mary School

 HOUGHTON MIFFLIN HARCOURT

PHOTOGRAPHY CREDITS: COVER ©George Grall/National Geographic/Getty Images; 3 (b) ©George Grall/National Geographic/Getty Images; 4 (b) ©Wildlife/Alamy Images; 5 (t) ©Getty Images; 6 (b) ©Iakov Kalinin/Fotolia; 7 (bl) ©William Leaman/Alamy Images; 7 (br) ©Nigel Cattlin/Alamy Images; 8 (b) ©pirita/Shutterstock; 9 (t) Brand X Pictures/Getty Images; 10 (t) ©Tim Mainiero/Shutterstock; 10 (inset) ©john a. shaw/Shutterstock; 11 (br) ©Vladimir Melnik/Shutterstock

If you have received these materials as examination copies free of charge, Houghton Mifflin Harcourt Publishing Company retains title to the materials and they may not be resold. Resale of examination copies is strictly prohibited.

Possession of this publication in print format does not entitle users to convert this publication, or any portion of it, into electronic format.

Copyright © by Houghton Mifflin Harcourt Publishing Company

All rights reserved. No part of this work may be reproduced or transmitted in any form or by any means, electronic or mechanical, including photocopying or recording, or by any information storage and retrieval system, without the prior written permission of the copyright owner unless such copying is expressly permitted by federal copyright law. Requests for permission to make copies of any part of the work should be addressed to Houghton Mifflin Harcourt Publishing Company, Attn: Contracts, Copyrights, and Licensing, 9400 Southpark Center Loop, Orlando, Florida 32819-8647.

Printed in Mexico

ISBN: 978-0-544-07256-5

5 6 7 8 9 10 0908 21 20 19 18 17 16 15 14

4500469985   A B C D E F G

Be an Active Reader!

Look at these words.

environment	food chain
pollen	adaptation

Look for answers to these questions.

What is an environment?
How do plants and animals depend on each other?
What is a food chain?
What adaptations help animals meet their needs?
What adaptations help plants meet their needs?

What is an environment?

Where do you live? What do you eat? Your home and your food are parts of your environment. All the living and nonliving things in a place make up an environment.

Plants and animals need air and water. They also need space to live and grow. Animals need shelter for protection. They need food to eat. These are all parts of their environments.

This woodpecker uses its strong beak to make a shelter in a tall tree.

How do plants and animals depend on each other?

Animals depend on plants for food and shelter. Deer feed on grass, flowers, and shrubs. Deer also sleep among trees. They hide in tall grass.

Beavers live on land and in water. They eat tree bark, twigs, leaves, and roots.

Beaver families live in lodges. They use nearby trees and mud to build these homes.

lodge

Beavers use logs and branches to make a lodge.

Butterflies carry pollen from flower to flower as they feed.

You have learned how animals use plants for food and shelter. Plants use animals, too. They use animals in a different way.

Watch a butterfly feed at a flower. The butterfly drinks a sweet liquid called nectar. As the butterfly drinks, a powder sticks to its body. The powder is called pollen.

The butterfly carries the pollen to the next flower it visits. The pollen rubs off on this second flower. The flower uses the pollen to make seeds.

What is a food chain?

Plants and animals link together in an important way. They make up a food chain. A food chain is the path that shows how energy moves from plants to animals.

Sunlight is part of the first step in any food chain. Plants use sunlight to make their own food.

step 1 in a food chain

Plants make their own food from sunlight.

Next, some animals, such as rabbits, eat grass and other plants. This is the second step in a food chain.

Other animals, such as hawks, eat the plant-eating animals. This is the third step in a food chain.

step 2 in a food chain

A rabbit eats grass.

step 3 in a food chain

A hawk eats the rabbit.

What adaptations help animals meet their needs?

Every environment is different. Animals have ways to survive where they live. These ways are called adaptations. An adaptation helps a living thing survive in its environment.

Horses eat grass and other plants. What adaptations help horses survive? Their strong, flat teeth grind their food so they can eat it.

Horses use their strong, flat teeth to eat grass.

Whales use flippers and a tail to travel through water.

What adaptations do animals need to live in water? A fish uses fins to swim and stay upright. The fins let the fish turn, stop, and steer through water.

Whales use flippers to steer through the water. They use a tail to push through the water.

If you see this poison ivy plant, stay away from it.

What adaptations help plants meet their needs?

Plants have adaptations, too. These adaptations protect plants against people and other animals.

Poison ivy makes a protective oil. The oil protects the plant from people and animals. If we are smart, we stay away from this plant. The oil will make your skin red and itchy.

Adaptations also let plants live in difficult environments. The Alaskan tundra is very cold for most of the year. How do plants live there?

Some tundra plants grow thick, hair-like parts. They protect the plants from the cold. Other tundra plants grow together in tight groups. Still others have dark colors. The dark colors let the plants take in heat from the sun.

These plants grow low to the ground to stay warm.

Responding

Make a Food Chain Poster

Go to a nearby garden or park. Work with a partner to find living things that might be part of the same food chain. Describe the food chain on a poster. Label each animal and plant. Write captions to describe how the animals and plants connect to each other.

Write a Letter

Write a letter to the editor of your school or classroom newspaper. Explain why you think the food chain you described in your poster is important. Read your letter aloud in class.